Hello, Family Members,

Learning to read is one of the most important accomplishments of early childhood. **Hello Reader!** books are designed to help children become skilled readers who like to read. Beginning readers learn to read by remembering frequently used words like "the," "is," and "and"; by using phonics skills to decode new words; and by interpreting picture and text clues. These books provide both the stories children enjoy and the structure they need to read fluently and independently. Here are suggestions for helping your child *before*, *during*, and *after* reading:

Before

- Look at the cover and pictures and have your child predict what the story is about.
- Read the story to your child.
- Encourage your child to chime in with familiar words and phrases.
- Echo read with your child by reading a line first and having your child read it after you do.

During

- Have your child think about a word he or she does not recognize right away. Provide hints such as "Let's see if we know the sounds" and "Have we read other words like this one?"
- Encourage your child to use phonics skills to sound out new words.
- Provide the word for your child when more assistance is needed so that he or she does not struggle and the experience of reading with you is a positive one.
- Encourage your child to have fun by reading with a lot of expression . . . like an actor!

After

- Have your child keep lists of interesting and favorite words.
- Encourage your child to read the books over and over again. Have him or her read to brothers, sisters, grandparents, and even teddy bears. Repeated readings develop confidence in young readers.
- Talk about the stories. Ask and answer questions. Share ideas about the funniest and most interesting characters and events in the stories.

I do hope that you and your child enjoy this book.

— Francie Alexander
Reading Specialist,
Scholastic's Learning Ventures

For Morgan Gruss Rosen
—K.M.

To Mom and Dad
—M.S.

Text copyright © 2001 by Kate McMullan.
Illustrations copyright © 2001 by Mavis Smith.
All rights reserved. Published by Scholastic Inc.
SCHOLASTIC, HELLO READER, CARTWHEEL BOOKS
and associated logos are trademarks and/or
registered trademarks of Scholastic Inc.

Library of Congress Cataloging-in-Publication Data

McMullan, Kate.
Fluffy meets the groundhog / by Kate McMullan ; illustrated by Mavis Smith.
p. cm. — (Hello reader! Level 3)
"Cartwheel books."
Summary: Groundhog Day inspires the class to celebrate Groundpig Day with their guinea pig Fluffy, and Fluffy gets to help an unhappy groundhog.
ISBN 0-439-20672-3
[1. Guinea pigs — Fiction. 2. Woodchuck — Fiction. 3. Groundhog Day — Fiction. 4. Schools — Fiction.] I. Smith, Mavis, ill. II. Title. III. Series.
PZ7.M2295 Ff 2001
[E] — dc21   00-035812

10 9 8 7   02 03 04 05

Printed in the U.S.A.   14
First printing, January 2001

MEETS THE GROUNDHOG

by Kate McMullan
Illustrated by Mavis Smith

Hello Reader! — Level 3

SCHOLASTIC INC.

Cartwheel
·B·O·O·K·S· ®

New York   Toronto   London   Auckland   Sydney
Mexico City   New Delhi   Hong Kong

The Groundhog

Ms. Day held up a picture
of an animal.

"Who knows what this is?" she asked.

"A squirrel?" said Maxwell.

"A muskrat?" said Emma.

"It's Fluffy!" said Wade.

"After he ate too
many carrots!"

I don't think so,
thought Fluffy.
Besides, who ever heard of
too many carrots?

"This is a groundhog,"
Ms. Day told the class.
"Tomorrow is Groundhog Day."
Fluffy looked at the picture of the groundhog.
It looked big and strong.
It looked very mean.

I am a very brave pig, thought Fluffy. But I hope I never meet a groundhog face to face.

"In the winter," said Ms. Day,
"a groundhog sleeps in its den.
On February second, winter is halfway over.
A legend says that the groundhog
wakes up on that day.
So we call February second, Groundhog Day."

Hey, I wake up every day,
thought Fluffy.
Why not name a day after me?

"The legend says that the groundhog can predict what the weather will be," said Ms. Day.

"Listen to this Groundhog Day poem.

If his shadow the groundhog spies,
Six more weeks of snow and ice.
If no shadow the groundhog sees,
Soon will blow a warm spring breeze."

"Can the groundhog really predict the weather?" asked Jasmine. **I don't believe a word of it,** thought Fluffy.

"If groundhogs can predict the weather,"
said Maxwell, "maybe guinea pigs can, too."
"Right!" said Jasmine.
"Our class should celebrate Groundpig Day!"
Everyone cheered.
Look out, Groundhog, thought Fluffy.
Make way for the Groundpig!

Groundpig Day

The next day, Ms. Day's class asked
Kiss, Duke, and Lucky Sue
to come and celebrate Groundpig Day.
Hey, thought Fluffy.
I thought this was MY holiday.

Today is Groundpig Day,
Fluffy told the other pigs.
We are the groundpigs.
Kiss said, **Not me.**
I'm a beautiful crested pig.

Everyone in Ms. Day's class
wrote a Groundpig Day poem.
Wade read his first.

If a groundpig runs fast,
Winter will not last.

Jasmine was next.

If a groundpig jumps up high,
To the winter say good-bye!

Emma and Maxwell wrote a poem together.

If a groundpig rolls on his back,
You can put your winter boots in a sack.

Ms. Day said, "I have a class full of poets!"

Groundpig Day was sunny
and very warm for February.
Ms. Day let the class
take the guinea pigs outside.
"Watch them carefully," said Ms. Day.
"We don't want any guinea pigs
running off."

We are groundpigs.

We have to look for our shadows,

Fluffy told the pigs again.

Says who? said Kiss.

I want to play tag.

She ran over and tagged Lucky Sue.

You're it! she cried.

Eeeeeee! said Lucky Sue. **I love to be it!**

She ran after Kiss.

Kiss jumped out of reach.

Lucky Sue tried to tag Duke.

But Duke rolled away just in time.

Hey, look at my cool shadow,

said Groundpig Fluffy.

But no one did.

"Lucky Sue is running fast," said Wade.

"That means winter won't last!"

"Look at Kiss jump,"

said Emma. "Good-bye winter!"

"Duke rolled over!" said Maxwell.

"We can pack up our winter boots."

I'm out of here,

thought Groundpig Fluffy.
And he took off.

Fluffy Meets the Groundhog

Fluffy looked back.

No one was running after him.

No one had even noticed he was gone.

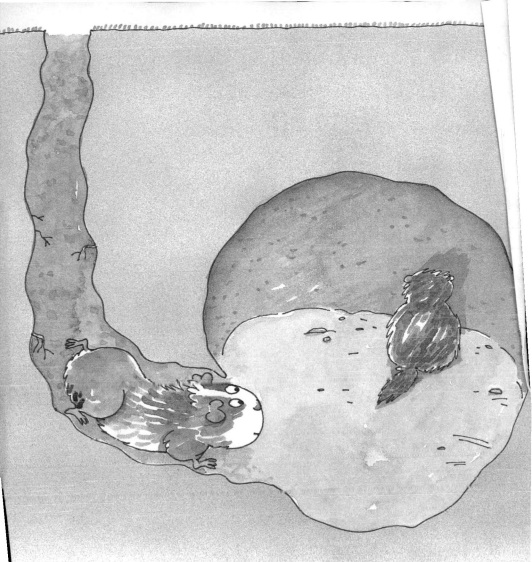

Down, down, down Fluffy crawled
through the dark tunnel.
At last he reached a den.
Fluffy thought he saw something move.
Yes! It was an animal!
Fluffy hoped the animal
would not turn around.

Fluffy came to a hole in the ground.
I will hide down here, thought Fluffy.
Soon everyone will miss me.
He crawled into the hole.

Very quietly,
he started up the tunnel.
But he tripped on a tree root
and fell back down.

The animal turned around.
Fluffy gasped!
He was face-to-face
with the groundhog!

The groundhog looked much meaner
than his picture.
**Why did you sneak in through
my back door?** he growled.

I was just leaving,
said Fluffy in a small voice.
Not so fast, said the groundhog.
Fluffy froze to the spot.

I'm sorry if I scared you,
said the groundhog.
You are? said Fluffy.
The groundhog nodded.
I'm having a bad day, he said.

But today is Groundhog Day,
said Fluffy.
You are a groundhog.
Doesn't that make it a good day?
The groundhog shook his head.
I am very shy, he said.

Hundreds of people are up there,
said the groundhog.
They are waiting to see me.
They have cameras.
They want to put my picture
in the newspaper. And on TV.
Oh, it is awful!

I have an idea, said Fluffy.

Groundpig Fluffy puffed himself up
to look big and strong.
He messed up his fur.
He practiced making a mean face.
Then he started up the tunnel
to the groundhog's front door.

Fluffy peeked out from
the groundhog hole.
He saw hundreds of people.
They had cameras. They were waiting.
Waiting for ME! thought Fluffy.
Just then a cloud
passed in front of the sun.

Fluffy popped out of the groundhog hole.

"There he is!" cried a reporter.

Flashbulbs started flashing.

TV cameras started rolling.

Fluffy looked to the right.

He looked to the left.

He even looked behind him.

But he did not see his shadow.

"Good news, folks!" said a reporter.

"The groundhog did not see his shadow.

Spring is on the way!"

Everyone clapped and cheered.

The groundpig took a bow.

Then he dove back into the hole.

Fluffy hurried back down to the den.
Nice work, said the groundhog.

Always glad to help out, said Fluffy.
Then he crawled up, up, up the tunnel
to the groundhog's back door.

Fluffy popped out of the hole.
"There he is!" yelled Maxwell.
He and Wade ran over to Fluffy
and picked him up.
"We thought you were lost," Wade said.
No way, thought Fluffy. **Not me.**

It was Wade's turn to take Fluffy
for the weekend.
His family got a big surprise that night
when they turned on the TV
to watch the news.
"Fluffy!" everyone cried.

The one and only!

thought Fluffy.

Happy Groundpig Day!